THE OLYMPICS ARE

Written and Illustrated

by

Graeme Mycko

Meet the animals, find their hidden clues and discover their dreams . . .

PELICAN BOOKS

Kelly Koala came down from her tree,
the Olympics were coming and she wanted to see
what all of her friends in the bush would be...

First she saw Flash, standing there by a stick.
Frill-neck Lizards are fast so Kelly had to be quick.

"The Olympics are coming and what will you be?"

"I think the SPRINTING is just right for me."
"Awesome!" said Kelly.

Vince the Wombat was easily found,
resting, as usual, by his hole in the ground.

"The Olympics are coming and what will you be?"

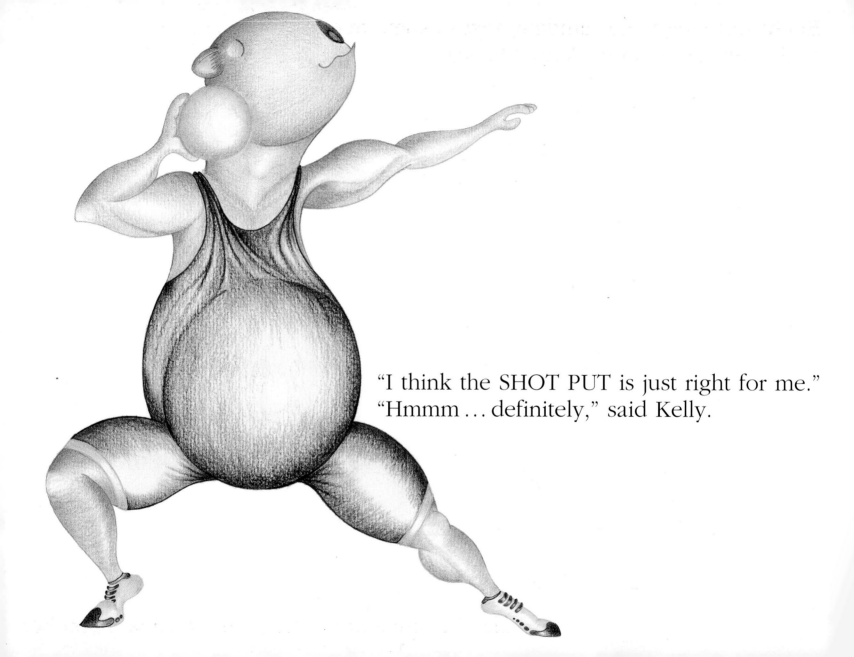

"I think the SHOT PUT is just right for me."
"Hmmm … definitely," said Kelly.

Emily and Joey were standing next to some trees,
Kelly only came up to Emily's knees.

"The Olympics are coming and what will you be?"

"I think the HIGH JUMP is just right for me."
"Me toooooo," said Joey.
"Wow, the Fosbury Flop!" said Kelly.

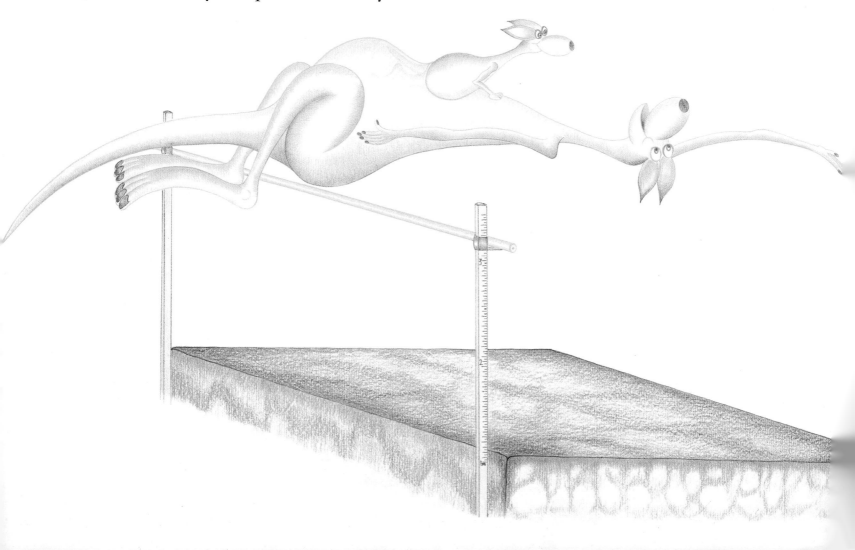

Next she met Leonard sitting under a palm,
the Dainty Green Tree Frog is quite cool and calm.

"The Olympics are coming and what will you be?"

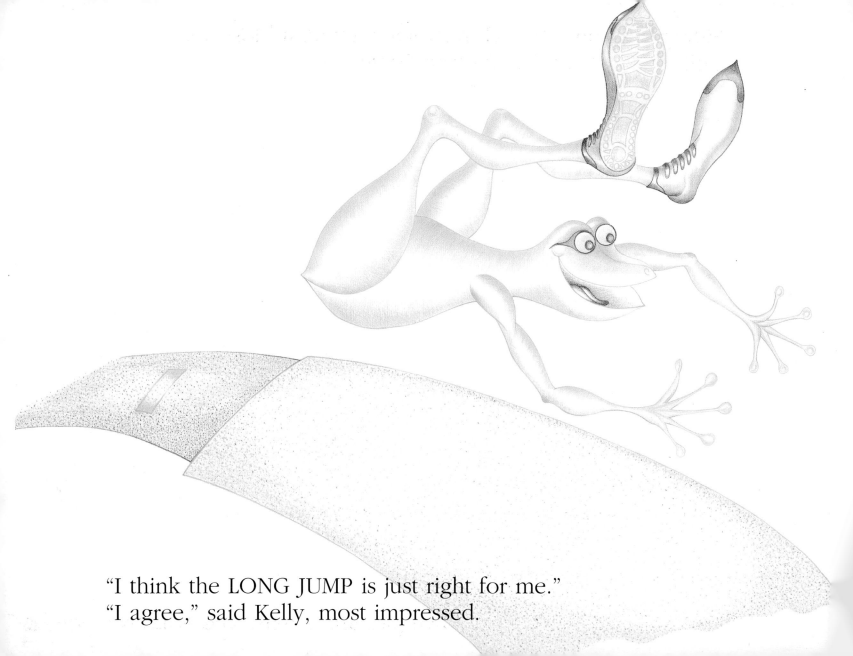

"I think the LONG JUMP is just right for me."
"I agree," said Kelly, most impressed.

Sitting high on a branch near some gumnut blossom,
Kelly found Peter the Ringtail Possum.

"The Olympics are coming and what will you be?"

"I think that BASKETBALL is just right for me."
"Superb!" exclaimed Kelly.

Ernie was busy looking around,
an Echidna gets hungry when ants can be found.

"The Olympics are coming and what will you be?"

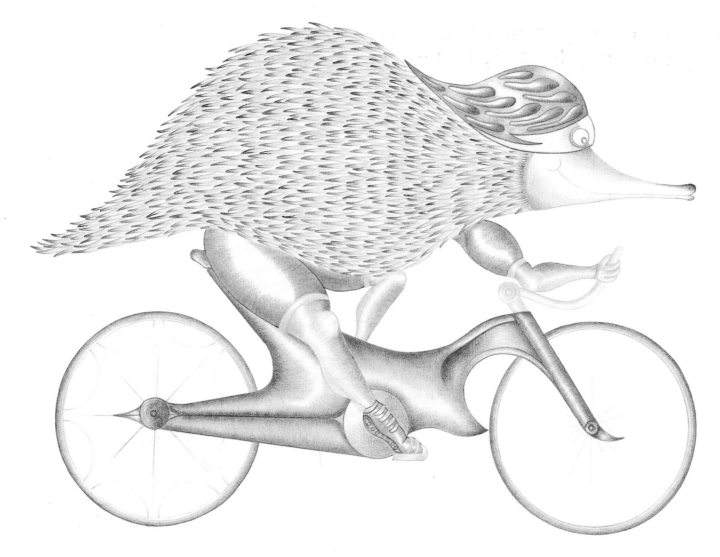

"I think the CYCLING is just right for me."
"Gosh!" said Kelly, as Ernie raced away.

When Elly the long-legged Emu walked past,
to keep up with Elly, Kelly had to move fast.

"The Olympics are coming and what will you be?"

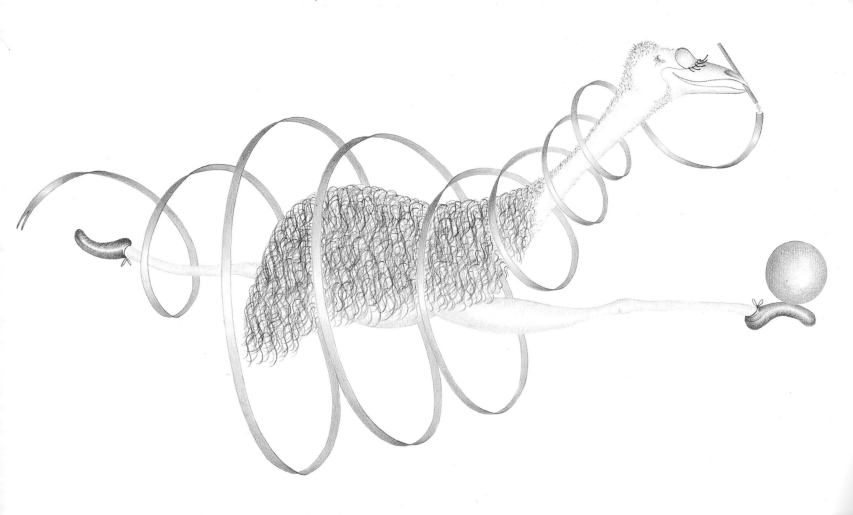

"I think RHYTHMIC GYMNASTICS is just right for me."
"A - mazing!" said Kelly.

Patricia the Platypus Kelly found in the reeds,
down by the pond where she usually feeds.

"The Olympics are coming and what will you be?"

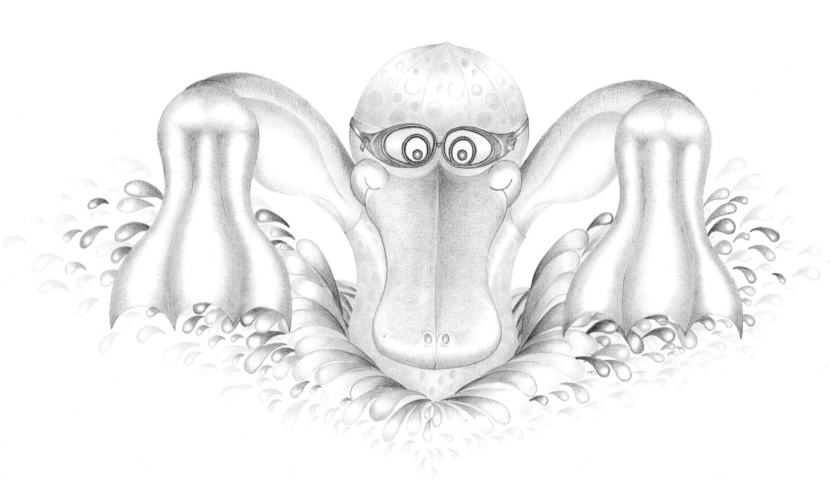

"I think the SWIMMING is just right for me."
"Absolutely," said Kelly.

Booka was waiting in the top of his tree.
This Kookaburra's smile is something to see.

"The Olympics are coming and what will you be?"

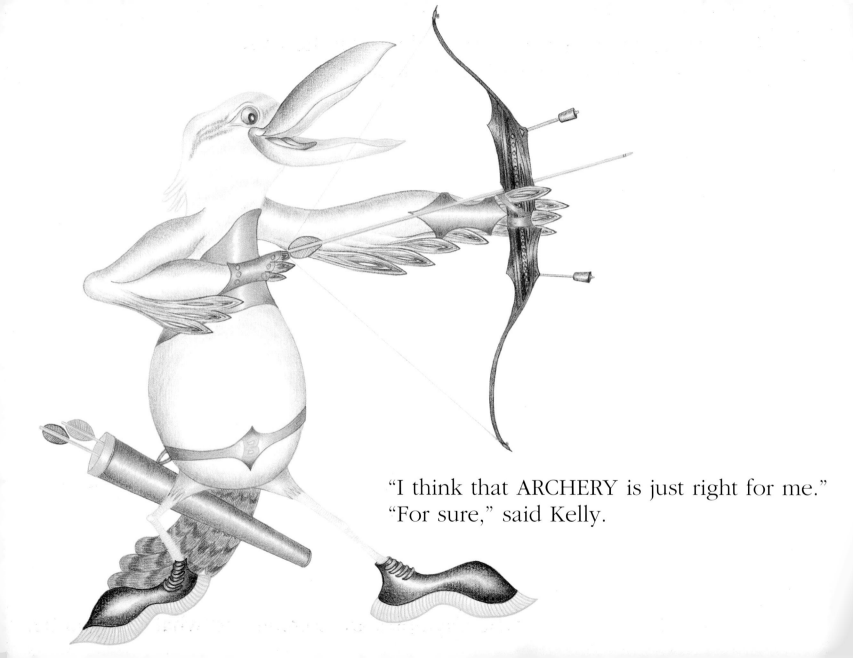

"I think that ARCHERY is just right for me."
"For sure," said Kelly.

Then while she was resting back down on the grass,
Erwin the Sulphur-crested Cocky strolled past.

"The Olympics are coming and what will you be?"

"I think the POLE VAULT is just right for me."
"Far out!" exclaimed Kelly.

Alfred was standing down by the creek.
This Long-necked Turtle looked cool, moist and sleek.

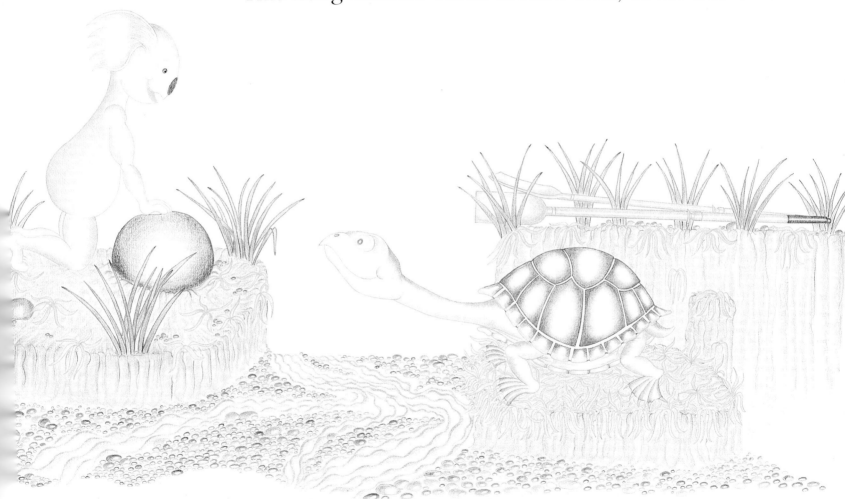

"The Olympics are coming and what will you be?"

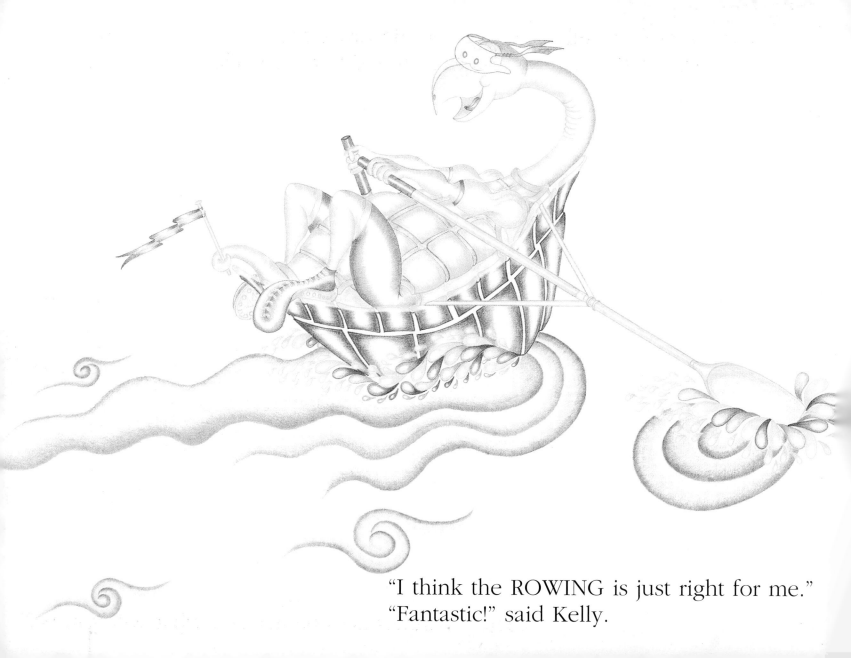

"I think the ROWING is just right for me."
"Fantastic!" said Kelly.

(From a distance) Kelly saw Gus the big Crocodile.
She'd heard all about crocs and their world-famous smile.

"The Olympics are coming and what will you be?"

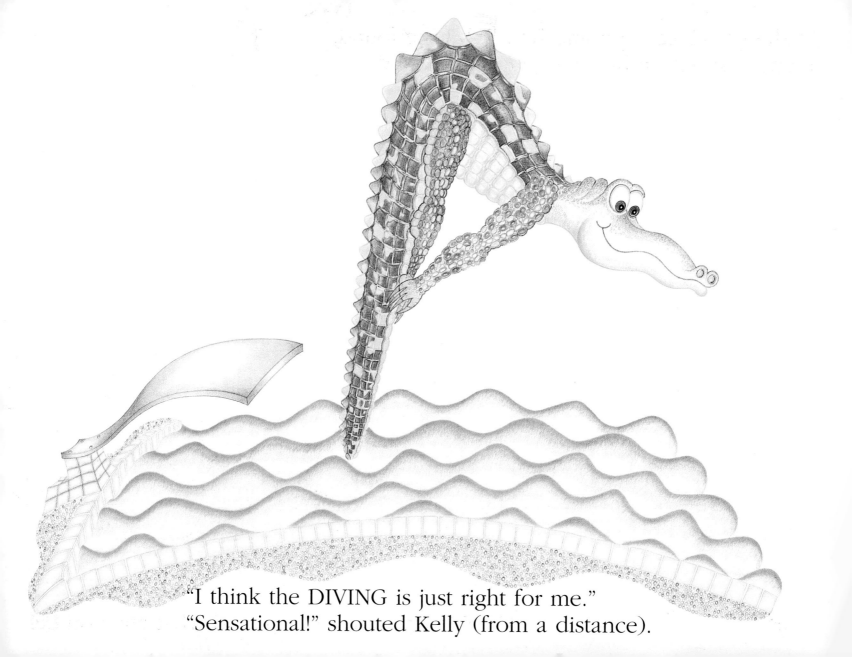

"I think the DIVING is just right for me."
"Sensational!" shouted Kelly (from a distance).

As she got closer to home Ben Bilby she found,
hopping about on his own patch of ground.

"The Olympics are coming and what will you be?"

"I think the WEIGHT-LIFTING is just right for me."
"Cool!" said Kelly.

When Kelly got home she thought of all the sports she had seen,
and was happy her friends were all very keen.

But the Olympics WERE coming and what could SHE be?

She would just have to TRY THEM ALL and see!

Published in 1999 by Pelican Books
PO Box 255, Semaphore SA 5019 AUSTRALIA
Phone/Fax (08) 8449 9819

Printed in Australia by Gillingham Printers Pty Ltd, Underdale, South Australia.
Graphics by Graf-X Pty Ltd, North Plympton, South Australia.

- With the Environment in mind we have chosen to use non-chemical
  based soya inks and paper which is 50% recycled and 50% oxygen bleached.

- With Children in mind, 20% of all profit made by Pelican Books are
  donated to Children's Hospitals and Schools throughout Australia.

- Thank you for choosing ⌐ Pelican Books.

National Library of Australia
Cataloguing-in-Publication data:
  Mycko, Graeme
  The Olympics are coming

  ISBN 0 646 37749 3

  1. Olympic Games (27th: 2000: Sydney, NSW) – Juvenile fiction.
  2. Olympics – Mascots – Juvenile fiction. I.

  A823.3